Little Red Riding Hood

Once upon a time, in a small village beside a forest, there lived a little girl and her mother. The little girl was always seen wearing a red, hooded cloak and came to be known as Little Red Riding Hood. The cloak was a gift from her beloved grandmother who lived in a cozy cottage in the woods.

One day, Little Red Riding Hood's mother asked her to do a very special task. Grandmother had recently fallen ill, and it was up to Little Red Riding Hood to bring her a basket of food her mother had prepared.

"Whatever you do, don't stray from the path!" warned her mother. "And no matter what happens, don't talk to strangers along the way!"

Little Red Riding Hood took the basket and merrily skipped off through the woods. It was a beautiful day, and she wasn't worried one bit.

A wolf spotted Little Red Riding Hood. He thought she looked quite tasty, but didn't dare pounce on her as there were woodcutters nearby.

"Where are you off to in such a hurry, little girl?" asked the prying wolf.

Little Red Riding Hood peered at the wolf. *He seems harmless enough*, she thought.

"I'm bringing this basket of food to my sick grandma. She lives all alone in a cozy cottage in the woods," she replied.

The wolf seized his opportunity.

"I know just the cottage," he replied. "I also know a shortcut that you can take. Just follow the path over there."

Little Red Riding Hood thought that was certainly a helpful tip.

"How kind of you, Mr. Wolf!" said Little Red Riding Hood. "Thanks for your help!"

Off she skipped down the other path.

As Little Red Riding Hood continued along her way, some beautiful wildflowers caught her eye.

I have plenty of time, she thought, as she stopped to pick a few. *A sweet-smelling bouquet will be just the thing to cheer up Grandma!*

Meanwhile, the wolf ran through the forest straight to Grandma's cozy cottage. He knew that it would be some time before Little Red Riding Hood arrived.

When the wolf arrived at the cottage, he knocked three times on the door and said in the sweetest voice he could muster, "It's me, Grandma, and I've brought you a basket of food! Can you please let me in?"

"Just lift the latch to let yourself in!" replied Grandma, too weak to get up.

The wolf entered the cottage to a very startled Grandma!
He sprang onto Grandma's bed and swallowed her up whole!

Next, the wolf put on Grandma's pajamas to disguise himself. Then, he climbed into Grandma's bed and pulled the blanket up to his chin to wait for Little Red Riding Hood.

Little Red Riding Hood finally arrived at Grandma's cottage and was surprised to see that the front door was wide open.

That's not like Grandma, she thought, but she entered the cottage all the same.

"Hi, Grandma!" said Little Red Riding Hood. "I hope you're feeling better today! I've brought you a basket of food from Mother and I picked you these flowers on my way here!"

"Just put everything on the table, sweetheart, and come closer where I can see you," said the wolf in his best Grandma voice.

Little Red Riding Hood noticed that her grandmother seemed a little strange, but decided that it must be her cold.

Little Red Riding Hood approached her bed cautiously.

"Oh, Grandma, what big ears you have!" she said.

"All the better to hear you with, my dear," replied the wolf.

Little Red Riding Hood crept closer for a better look.

"Oh, Grandma, what big eyes you have!" she said, surprised.

"All the better to see you with, my dear," croaked the wolf.

"Oh, Grandma, what big teeth you've got!" gasped the little girl.

"All the better to eat you up with!" growled the wolf.

In an instant, the wolf sprang onto Little Red Riding Hood and swallowed her up whole!

Feeling extremely full after two very satisfying meals, the wolf fell sound asleep.

A huntsman passing by the cottage heard very loud snoring coming from Grandma's window.

That's funny, he thought.

He decided to check to see that everything was alright.

He opened the cottage door and was shocked! Lying on Grandma's bed, dressed in her clothes, was a snoring wolf with a great big belly!

The huntsman recognized the wolf at once. It was the very same wolf who had been stealing all the little lambs from the village! Every time he was caught, the clever wolf would find a way to escape. The huntsman knew he had to act quickly in order to save Grandma and be rid of this beast for good!

The huntsman decided not to wake the wolf. He carefully cut open the sleeping wolf's belly, and was quite surprised by what he found. Out jumped not only Grandma, but Little Red Riding Hood, too!

Little Red Riding Hood and her grandmother were so happy to be saved! They hugged each other tightly and thanked the huntsman for his bravery. They invited him to share the basket of food.

I'll certainly think twice about talking to strangers from now on! Little Red Riding Hood thought to herself.

They all lived happily ever after, and the wolf never bothered anyone ever again.